Prince Percy and the Big Red Ruby

by Jenny Phillips

Illustrated by McKenzie Rose West

Chapter 1

Percy was a prince. He lived in a tall castle on a hill. The castle was lovely with white and gray stones that glittered in the sun.

The inside of Percy's castle was fancy. Blue satin curtains framed the windows.

Fancy dishes were used.

The chairs were made from dark carved wood and green velvet.

His library had many books.

The castle had fifty rooms.
Here are some of them.

One of the greatest things about Percy's castle was the castle grounds. There were hundreds of bushes and trees. There was even a maze made with shrubs.

The castle grounds had five huge fountains. This fountain was Percy's favorite one.

The birds loved it, too.

Percy's castle had a huge stable with forty horses. This was Percy's horse. It was light brown with white spots, and it had a white mane.

Percy even had a beautiful peacock. It strutted around and showed off its tail.

Percy was a little bit like the peacock. He strutted around proudly, feeling important in his fancy clothes and golden crown.

Percy thought he was too good to be friends with the children in town.

The king and queen were very sad. They loved Percy, but they could see that he was very smug and selfish.

One day they watched Percy out the window turning his nose up while a baker was bringing his cart to the castle.

"Oh," sighed the king. "I wish there were a way to make Percy more kind. Surely we have spoiled him!"

Chapter 2

One day Percy went out to the hills to have a picnic with his tutor and two guards.

What a feast! This is what the picnic looked like.

The clouds floated lazily in the sky. The breeze was cool. The bees hummed. Soon, the guards and tutor all fell asleep on the soft grass.

Percy did not fall asleep.
He saw the cool shadows of a
nearby forest.

"I'll just explore the forest for
a few minutes," thought Percy.
"I'll be back before my tutor or
the guards awaken. I want to
see what the forest is like."

And with those thoughts,
he walked into the forest
and found a path that wound
through the tall trees.

The forest was calm and cool

and full of the sounds of birds.
In the big forest, Percy felt
small.

Clouds began to cover the sky, and the forest became more dim. Percy was scared. Then he heard a noise in the bushes ahead of him. Out jumped a little fawn.

The cute animal looked like it knew where it was going, so Percy followed it.

The fawn began to run, so Percy began to run. Before long, Percy realized he was no longer on the path. He was deep in the forest and could no longer see the fawn.

Things got even worse! A rumble of thunder sounded in the distance. In a panic, Percy began to run again.

Blinded by tears and rain that had started to sprinkle, Percy could not see well. He tripped over a fallen branch and tumbled down a long hill.

His velvet cape came off. His clothes ripped. Mud splattered all over his body.

Down, down he went, landing with a splash in a river. Poor Percy! He grabbed onto a floating log and began yelling for help.

Just then, out of the corner of his eye, Percy saw movement. Two children, a boy and a girl about his age, were running along the river bank.

With a flying leap, the boy

skillfully dove into the river.
Within moments, the boy had
pulled Percy to the bank.

Percy lay on the bank
panting and groaning. He did
not even think to thank the
boy.

Chapter 3

Once Percy recovered, he stood up and faced the two children. "Take me back to the castle," he demanded.

"The castle!" cried the boy. "It's miles and miles away. The sun will be setting soon. You could not get halfway to the castle before dark."

"I don't care; I'll travel in the dark," said Percy. "I'm the prince, and I demand to be taken home now."

The two children looked surprised. Percy certainly did not look like a prince at the moment with his ripped, dirty, wet clothes.

"There are wolves at night," said the girl gently. "You had better follow us home."

Just then, a strong wind picked up, and it began to sprinkle again. The girl put her hand on Percy's shoulder.

"I only talk to important people," said Percy.

"Good," said the girl. "We are important. Follow us, and we'll get you dry and warm. We'll get you some dinner, too."

The two children started walking away. Percy looked at their clothing. It was not fancy, but it was well made. The girl's hair was twisted in beautiful braids on her head with little white flowers dotting her hair here and there.

"Perhaps they are important," thought Percy. His stomach rumbled with hunger, and he shivered as he started to follow the children.

"I'm Robin," said the boy, "and this is my twin sister, Daisy. You must be Prince Percy. What happened to bring you here?"

"I lost my way; that's all," said Percy shortly.

In a few minutes, the group came to the edge of a very wide river.

"Here's our raft; hop on," said Daisy.

Percy did not want to get on the raft, but he had nowhere else to go, so he stepped onto the raft and sat huddled up. Robin started moving the raft with a long paddle.

Thunder rumbled, and the wind whistled across the choppy water.

When they finally landed on the other side of the river, Daisy quickly tied the raft to a wooden pole.

"Look at those clouds!" cried Daisy. "This is going to be quite a storm. We need to hurry home. Let's run!"

"I will not run," said Percy as he put his nose in the air. But just then, lightning cut through the sky, and cold, slanted sheets of rain began to pour from the clouds.

Percy ran.

It wasn't long until a cottage came into view with windows aglow with golden light.

A kind-looking man got up from the table. "I was so worried about you two. Who do you have with you?"

"Father," said Robin, "this is Prince Percy. He has lost his way. We found him and invited him home."

"You are most welcome, Prince Percy. I am John," said the man.

Percy barely nodded a hello. "Your children told me you were important," stated Percy, looking doubtfully around the room. "I can see that they were not truthful."

"Ah," replied the man with a twinkle in his eye. "They were most truthful. Not only are we important, but we are rich, indeed. I will explain later. For now, let's get you three warmed up and fed."

Percy felt strange as he sat by the warm fire, wrapped in a blanket, sipping steaming stew from a wooden bowl.

He had never eaten simple stew from a wooden bowl before, yet he felt that perhaps he had never enjoyed a meal quite so much.

John could see how tired the poor boy was. He showed him to Robin's bed in the loft. Percy stomped his foot and refused to sleep there, but when he realized there was nowhere else to sleep, he crawled under the quilt.

Once again, he felt strange as

he looked out the loft window, watching the trees bending in the strong wind and listening to the constant patter of the rain on the wooden roof. He had never heard rain on a roof before. He had never slept with a patchwork quilt. He had never . . . fallen asleep so quickly.

Chapter 4

The night had chased away the storm. Golden sunbeams moved across the room and warmed Percy's cheek. He sat up in bed with a start.

"Who will get me dressed?" he wondered. "Who will bring me my breakfast?"

The room was still and silent. Then Percy heard noises outside. Leaning out the window, Percy saw Robin, Daisy, and their father doing morning chores.

"I'm hungry!" called Percy.

John called up to him. "Good morning, Prince Percy! Why don't you get dressed and come join us! There is some bread and butter on the table for your breakfast."

Percy went and sat on his bed. "Bread and butter?" thought Percy. "I want poached eggs and cinnamon pancakes, not bread. Also, I have never dressed myself."

Dressing himself was a bit of a struggle, but he figured it out and went downstairs to eat his bread and butter.

Dressed in rumpled clothes, Percy presented himself to the family.

"It's time for you to take me home, and you shall be punished for lying to me."

"Lying?" asked Daisy.

"Yes, you said you were rich," replied Percy.

"Ah," said John. "We are rich."

"Humph!" said Percy. "At home, I have a ruby as big as my fist. It's the biggest ruby in the world. That is just *one* of the many jewels I have. What riches do you have? I don't see anything of value here."

"I think," said John, "that you would be amazed at what we have. Come, let me show you."

Percy followed John. From under his bed, John pulled out a locked wooden box.

"In here is something that I feel is more valuable than your ruby, but I won't show it to you right now. You must first learn wisdom."

Percy demanded three times that John open the box. John would not.

"Then take me home!" said Percy.

"Very well," said John. Soon, John had a wagon hooked up to his horses, and the family was on their way to the castle. Percy sat proudly in the wagon as they crossed the great stone bridge across the river.

Back at the castle, Percy stared at his ruby. He took it with him to eat dinner. He even slept with it.

"No one has such a great jewel as this!" he said.

But, the truth is, he was thinking about something more than the ruby; it was John's wooden box.

What if there were something greater in that box? If so, Percy thought he should have it.

He convinced his father, the king, to assemble forty soldiers.

On white horses, with shields and swords shining in the sun, the soldiers dashed over the green hills toward John's home.

With Percy riding on a horse behind a soldier, they dashed across the great bridge.

Chapter 5

When forty soldiers dashed into Daisy's yard, she screamed and dropped the bucket she was carrying. John and Robin came running.

Percy jumped from the horse. "The wooden box!" he said with his chin in the air. "It belongs to me. Only a prince should own such a great treasure."

He sent his soldiers into the home to get the box.

Percy would not listen to Daisy's or Robin's pleadings.

With the box securely in a basket on a horse, Percy rode away with the soldiers.

Another storm was gathering. The clouds were blacker than any other clouds Percy had seen. The air grew suddenly cold, and a strong wind whipped through the forest. A huge gust of wind bent a branch, and it knocked Percy off the back of his horse.

No one saw Percy fall.

The wind was roaring so
loudly that no one heard
Percy's call as he lay on the
forest floor. He was not hurt,
but he was *mad*! He got up and

ran after the horses just as the rain started to pour.

Never had Percy seen rain like this. It came down in sheets, and rivulets ran through the forest. Percy was sure the little waterfalls he saw everywhere had not been in the forest that morning.

After an hour, he finally reached the great stone bridge, or . . . what was left of it.

The river had swollen so

high that it had broken the bridge into pieces. Percy fell on his knees in fear as the rain continued to pour. He knew that no soldier could cross the river to save him.

Remembering there were wolves in the forest, Percy decided he must go back to Daisy and Robin's home, the only safe place he knew of in these woods.

He ran along the path as the sun sank lower and lower. Panting and nearly out of strength, he could no longer run. He walked, and his walking became slower and slower. The sun disappeared behind the trees, and the moon climbed into the dark sky but was hidden behind the clouds.

A wolf's howl in the distance got Percy running fast again. Finally, he saw a light in the distance. What a relief!

When he arrived at the cottage, the rain was still pouring. He pounded on the door. When it opened, he fell inside the cottage, his strength totally gone.

Chapter 6

Percy slept half of the next day. When he awoke, he demanded to be taken home. However, the bridge was destroyed, and the river raged too strongly to take the raft across.

"It looks like you are stuck here until the river calms down," said John. "That could be several days or even weeks."

The rain kept drizzling for days. Percy, refusing to do any work, became utterly bored. There was one thing he enjoyed—a painting hanging in the kitchen. He had not noticed it the last time he had come.

In this painting a lone cottage sat atop stately ocean cliffs, and a group of white seagulls flew against dark storm clouds. The waves crashed into rocks at the base of the cliff, creating majestic white spray. A father and daughter were walking on a winding path through deep green fields dotted with white sheep.

As Percy sat and stared at the painting, he felt something he never had noticed feeling before—peace. He wished he could be at the place in the painting.

"I've never been to the sea before," he said to Daisy one day. "Where is this place in the painting?"

"That is where my mother grew up," replied Daisy. "It's in the next kingdom over."

Percy jumped up. "Tall Towers Kingdom—the kingdom of our enemies? Your mother belongs to that kingdom?"

"Yes," replied Daisy.

"And where is your mother?"

Daisy sighed. "That is a very long story."

"Please tell it to me," said Percy, not realizing he had said "please" for the first time in his life.

Percy sat by the crackling fire on a soft sheepskin as the rain drizzled outside.

Daisy began, "My mother grew up in Tall Towers

Kingdom. Like I said, she lived in the cottage shown in the painting. In fact, she is the one who made that painting."

"She's an artist?" asked

Percy, enthralled with the story already.

"Yes, she is a wonderful artist. The king of Tall Towers wanted her to live at the castle and paint pictures of him and the royal family. My mother, however, wanted to paint nature, not the king. When he said he would force her to live at the castle, she ran away—to our kingdom.

She met my father, and we lived in this far-off cottage so

she would not be found. But eventually, a few months ago, she was found and captured. She is being held prisoner by the king of Tall Towers Kingdom."

A single tear slid down Daisy's cheek. "I miss her so much," she said.

Chapter 7

Percy did not sleep well. All night he was thinking of Daisy's mother. It made him think of his own mother and how he missed her.

However, he shouted for joy when he saw the blue sky outside his window that morning. The clouds and the rain had finally disappeared.

At breakfast John said, "I

wish we could take you home, Percy, but the river will still be too swollen all week."

Just then, Daisy dropped her fork and pointed out the window. "What is that?" she cried.

Percy turned around and looked. "Oh, oh, oh! It is Father's hot air balloon. He has come to get me."

And it was true.

The magnificent gold and

blue balloon landed in a nearby field. The king stepped out, and Percy ran to him and hugged him—a very rare thing. Percy never hugged anyone.

Within ten minutes, Percy was sailing away. Daisy, Robin, and John waved.

The land looked beautiful to Percy as they flew over the green hills. When he got home to the castle, his mother was waiting for him. Percy never really noticed before how

beautiful and kind his mother looked. He ate lunch with her and told her all about his adventure.

Then Percy went to his room. There, sitting on his elegant bed, was John's wooden box. He had forgotten all about it.

Suddenly, he did not really want the box anymore. He was a little scared to open it. Over on his dresser stood another box—the one that held his ruby.

"Hmmm," he thought, "John did say that there was a treasure more valuable than my ruby. I would like to know what it is. Maybe I will give it back after I see it."

Slowly Percy lifted the lid of the flat box. Inside was a square painting. He held it up. It was a family portrait with Daisy, Robin, John, and . . . their mother.

She had dark curly hair and the same kind of beautiful smile that Daisy had. She was holding Daisy's and Robin's hands.

For a few minutes, Percy
stared at the beautiful
painting.

"A treasure greater than
a ruby?" Percy thought. "A
loving family. Is that greater

than the biggest ruby in the world?"

Something pricked Percy's mind and heart as he looked at the painting and then at the ruby. He felt there was an important plan somewhere in the back of his mind that he had to think of.

Percy thought hard. It hurt his head because he was not used to thinking about anything other than himself.

He tried thinking upside down.

He tried thinking while sitting in a tree.

"I've got it!" he said. "I must help Daisy and Robin get their mother back."

Chapter 8

So Percy went to his father, the king, and asked what could be done.

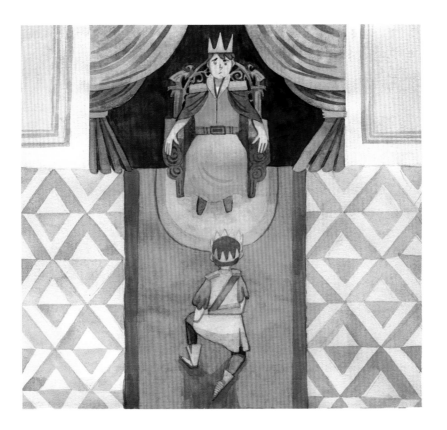

The king frowned and said, "The king of Tall Towers Kingdom is our bitter enemy. He would never release Daisy's mother if I asked him."

"Father, why is he our bitter enemy?" Percy asked.

The king sighed. "Your ruby, Percy. When you were a little boy, you demanded to have the biggest ruby in the world. You kicked and yelled for a week. Finally, I asked the king of Tall Towers if I could buy the ruby. He refused. It had belonged to his mother, and he would not sell it for any price. So . . . so . . . well . . . um, I ordered an army of my soldiers to go take it by force. We have been enemies ever since."

"Oh," said Percy. He felt very, very, very sad. He did not like that feeling, so he tried to push it away by doing other things.

He ate a big meal with fancy foods. He went swimming in his fancy pool with waterfalls and fountains. Still, the sad feeling stung his heart.

Finally, Percy went to his room and looked in his mirror. What he saw was a boy that looked like a peacock. He did not want to look like a peacock. He wanted to have the same kind of happy, friendly faces as Daisy and her family. But how?

Percy saw the ruby sitting on his dresser. Suddenly, he knew what to do. Grabbing the ruby, he ran to the king's throne.

"Father," cried Percy. "It was wrong for the king of Tall Towers to take Daisy's mother. We were wrong, as well, in stealing his ruby. I want to give it back to him personally and apologize."

The king looked at Percy with his jaw dropped and eyes wide open. Finally, he smiled. "Yes, we

should do that. We'll leave first thing tomorrow."

The next day dawned bright and beautiful. The river glittered like a thousand diamonds as Percy and his father set off with only two of their soldiers.

The king of Tall Towers was overjoyed to have his ruby back. When Percy told the king about his friends, Daisy and Robin, and how much they missed their mother, the king's heart was touched.

Percy and his father had
the privilege of bringing
Daisy's mother back home and
watching the joyful reunion.

Years later, can you guess what happened? Prince Percy married Daisy. The wedding

was held by the beautiful ocean
cliffs near the place where
Daisy's mother grew up.

Though Prince Percy still had peacocks, he never again acted like one. He became a kind man who loved to serve all those around him.

The End